Evincepub Publishing

Evincepub Publishing

Parijat Extension, Bilaspur, Chhattisgarh 495001
First Published by Evincepub Publishing 2021
Copyright © S.Siangshai 2021
All Rights Reserved.

ISBN: 978-93-5446-034-0

The Journey Of An Imaginary's Mind

S. SIANGSHAI

O sparkling bitter tears

O sparkling morning dew

Are Stars made out of you?

Acknowledgment

Throughout the journey of writing this poetry book, I will like to express my gratitude towards Anxiety, Emotions, Solitude, Sadness, Happiness, Love, and Art itself in all its forms, that has greatly inspired and irrigated me with my writings. Pray they all are considerate enough so I can have another poetry book.

Also I will like to thank my mother and dear friend Hage Apa.

Contents

S. Siangshai

The Night

The night is here,
Crickets to the ear.
The moon shines bright
Leaving no being to fright.

Far from the bustle-maddening crowd
Where only night creatures sound loud.
The calm sky is clear,
Nature being quite a dear.

All the evil's asleep
No worries left to keep.
All the pain ceases
For a moment, there is peace.

Let the night go at a slow pace
For this is something to embrace.

Mother

Mother, a tree in the family,
Sheltering us from the wind and rain—
A resting place providing shade—
'Comfort to our disturbed minds and pain.
She spreads love through her roots
For us to bear those fruits.

Mother, a strong, standing tree—
Shedding leaves of affection, endlessly free.
The bright light in the dark,
In our hearts, you are but a spark.

Mother, a burning candle in the darkness—
Consuming herself for our happiness.

S. Siangshai

If only

If only you were mine,
Together will always dine,
With a bottle of sweet red wine,
To keep the silence fine.

If only you were a true lover,
And not a witty deceiver,
We'd water each other
So, our love would never wither
And we'd grow old together.
We'd define the word 'Forever',
But you're only an imaginary, reflected stranger.

Conflicting Thoughts

System ruled by fear
Nothing now is clear.
Government says obey or jail—
School says to obey or fail—
Religion says obey or hell;
Placing into our mind a strong spell.
Some feel educated,
Without realizing being indoctrinated.

Corrupted politics controls the sheep;
To the unconscious ones their power creeps.
Slowly depriving the individual's Freedom—
Brainwashed to follow the set-up decorum.

Wings clipped, voice shut, in a cage;
While conflicting disputes thoughts in rage.

S. Siangshai

When She

When she passes by,
Even the trees sigh,
Feelings jump to fly,
Merely reaching a nigh.

When she stares and smiles,
Even strangers stop and gaze awhile.
And I fall faster than the autumn leaves
In pursuit of hopeless, romantic, ephemeral
beliefs.

When she gives a gloomy glance,
Even the moon shies to shine.
Caught up again in this romance,
I'm trying to perfect each line.

Memories of the Past

Came home wearily—
The air cold and pale, blew drearily—
Sadness hit heavily—
An innocent soul was lost tragically—
As she left the house in melancholy;
The hut's fire went off swiftly—
Darkness lurked in frightfully—
Neither the stars now shine brightly.

Lay in peace now forever,
Every spring you'll have a flower,
Not from thy lover
But from thy true love mother.

Time may run fast
But not memories of the past.

S. Siangshai

Grandmother's Tale

One fine morning, a boy sat by the window,
Pulled the curtain to watch the Sun rise slow.
A sibling came stumbling, half-asleep,
And pulled another curtain to peep.

Silent and calm, without any sound,
Both favored, the tree's dead, withered leaves fell
to the ground.

The fire in the cot burned fondly still;
Beside it, sat a cat, coldly ill.

Far in the distance, from underneath the
mountains,
The Sun rose in a yellow-reddish color.
Then a cloud, in a frog's form,
Drifted towards the Sun,
Slowly, it started consuming the source of light;
This darkened the sky and barely produced sight.

An hour passed, the boy still gazed
With less hope, he waited for the sunrise.
He remembered old grandmother — wrinkled
and pale;
And recalled the scene had been from one of her
great tales.

Nature's cry

Sat by the window,
Watched Nature cry like a widow.

Wind blows,
River flows,
Thunderstruck,
Trees and flowers duck.

What's more beautiful?
Is feeling blissful —
At the moment.

In the midst of Nature

In the midst of nature, in spring
Often times, I'll find myself woolgathering.

With the sound of the creek running,
Sweet melodies of the birds chirping,
A soft gentle breeze passing,
The bees humming to the scent of flowers,
O, these sounds have lulled my soul, many times.

Mesmerized by the beauty of nature —
Caught up in the divinity of rapture —
I'm lost in reverie, musing.

The Rain Poured and Poured

The rain poured and poured
Mud wetted and soured.
A month goes by, still dripping, pattering
Dark clouds moving—
Wind whooshing—
Waterfalls gushing—
Thunder and lightning, flickering lights.

Electric went off
Everyone is left a blind to the blackness at
night—
With only a bare blurry sight.

In the midst all that
Thoughts and voices in the head gone wild
Sickening and frightening.
Silent in solitude
And yet, it's deafening.

Carried Away

Alone,
Staring at the blue sky
And white clouds,
Fantasizing myself fly
Or hover among the clouds —
Swiftly moving as directed by the wind,
And gently carried away into the celestial sky.
I am set free,
With little moments of glee,
I felt a little carefree.
Floating, floating,
Until reality hit me, drowning.

Humming in Melancholy comes the Wind

Humming in melancholy comes the wind,
Blowing from the sea,
Raised by voiceless creatures —
In praise of some sorrowful stories.
Swiftly moving, carrying the sweet melancholic tune,
Leaving a few in solitude —
With nostalgic memories of their lost childhood,
And deeply gripped by the soft tune and blue evening mood.

Humming in melancholy comes the wind,
A sweet soothing tune to the mind —
A wanderer that brings a lonely outraged man to a calm —
A long lost tune, a soothing balm.

S. Siangshai

The Lost Song

She reaps and reaps,
On the field, with parched tongue and dry lips,
Looking somewhat strange, mysterious and
tragically deep,
As her tears rolled down her cheeks and slowly
dripped.

She sings the sweetest melody,
Of some ancient heart-touching song;
A song of battle 'bout a lady
That was once helpless and still stood strong.

Her sweet voice echoed in the *air most sweet*;
Can touch the heart of any passerby, hearing it.
A lullaby to any sleepless child;
Morphine to a sick man with thoughts gone wild.

Beside the field, a shepherd with his pipe;
Played along with the song of a lady in distress,
Producing a sweetly-sad music type,
While his cattle graze upon the dying grass.

Such pleasing sound, I've never heard,
From a fair lady and a shepherd.
A lulling melody, to a vagabond like me,
Lying under a willow tree.

When the Sun has set

When the sun has set,
And all the shepherds
Have driven home with all their herds,
Two little boys and a pet
Head home slowly, climbing a hill
As darkness takes over the joyous day.
The only light that guides their way,
Is the bright moon standing still.

With tired feet, they walk wearily,
And a little behind, the pet follows,
With less strength, he has become slow.
They were all thirsty and hungry.
Eager to get home, they hurry
As they think of food,
And hope their parents are in a good mood.

As they reach near their house,
They find their only house on fire.
The pet growls as to grouse,
While they break into sadness,
As they find themselves now homeless.

S. Siangshai

A Dream

Boom! Crash!
At midnight
I hit the streetlight
The night had been doomed and gloomed.

Death flash before my eyes
And all my worldly lies —
Ready to confess for forgiveness.

I laid there bleeding
In the drizzling rain
Numb to all the pain.

Five spirit wanderers came by
Asked me to bid goodbye—
To my fragile impermanent vessel
And be united with my beloved damsel.

Next thing I know
 My body, in the funeral pyre
Burned slowly under the fire
As the wind blow.

Remember me

Remember me
When it drizzles on a sunny day
As you find your way
 Back to me.

Remember me
When the soft breeze comes in slow,
And your face starts to glow
As you imagine me
Holding you.

When the sun has set,
And you feel like a lost pet,
Remember me,
And *look up at the sky,*
And say your last goodbye.

A Red Bird

There's this red bird, cut off of his wings,
He now only sings
With a sad and sorrowful tone
As he hides his rage within his bones,
All by himself, alone.

He's had no luck,
Life itself has become a rock.
He is now stranded, forlorn,
Who persists to go on
As he hopes for better days,
And the world to be a better place.

In love with a coma patient

Her eyes bright like stars,
Her smiles like glowing sunshine,
Her touch as tender as a feather,
Her voice as sweet as a Nightingale's.

What secrets lie between those eyes?
A riddle I can never handle.
What are the reasons for the rejection?
A dejection I can never reason.

If my heart could speak,
It would tell you
How heartless you are.

How can you be so consciously unaware?
How can you not care?
Why are you insensibly mute?
O, but then I forget
I'm in love with a coma patient.

S. Siangshai

Untitled

Corrupted leaders,
Corrupted followers,
Corrupted, bribed voter,
Look now, where we are.

Betrayed by our own Representatives,
Betrayed by the Government,
Our own land about to overturn,
And our heritage and culture about to burn.

Internet shutdown,
Freedom of expression is suppressed.
A protest —
A revolt —
Fire —
Smoke —
Gunshots —
Bodies on the ground,
Shoot not a Civilian,
But a Judas' Politician.

Waiting to be found

Here I am, as I stand still —
With heavy feelings to deal,
Lost in between somewhere and nowhere,
Which I really do not care.
I watch people come and go,
As I keep up with the flow.

All I see is busy people
Who are all in a state of misery.

In childhood, I was taught
To stand still and wait
If I ever got lost —
Till someone found me.

And so, here I am, standing still
With a weary heart and heavy sound,
Waiting to be found
By someone who'll make me astound.

S. Siangshai

Farewell Love

Farewell Love
To all those good times,
And the coquet lines,
And rhymes,
I ever wrote to you.
To all those starry nights,
We both enjoyed without any fights.
To those little moments of ethereal,
That now have become surreal.
And to those coquettish smiles,
That made me go the extra miles.

Farewell Love,
To all those summer days,
When we both used to gaze,
Up at the beautiful sky,
And how we both wished to fly.

Farewell Love,
To all those romantic enchanted days,
And your angelic moves in mysterious ways,
That deluded me into falling for you.

And to all those touches,
That gave a taste of ecstasy.
Those temporary romances
Are now but a glance.

Farewell Love,
For all those flashes of our past
Have turned to dust and ashes,
I do not wish them to last.
This is Goodbye,
Let all our memories now die.

S. Siangshai

The Cry of a Sheep

"Examinations only test our speed;
Not thoroughly our knowledge."

Routines to follow - in our head,
Every morning - no time for bread,
Running to assemble while half asleep,
Standing in line like a flock of lost sheep.

Closed, contained, we remained and stayed,
Following a set of rules like fools.

Some teachers like to speak and preach,
About the role of a teacher,
And yet still lack the skill to teach.
They speak of a student-teacher relationship
But build that only with their favorite sheep.

The institution has made our brains dull
And left our vision blurred.
Few are educated, many are left indoctrinated.

We're a flock of sheep, who've lost our creativity,
To the institution with less productive activity.

You did not fail me, mother.
You see, it's the System, Institution
And Education
That failed me altogether.

S. Siangshai

Winter's Beauty

What a lovely, lovely day
To gaze at nature and be amazed.
It is that time of the year
When the leaves die without fear.
The wind of longing
Comes and takes away happiness;
But sometimes sadness too,
With its sweet and nostalgic smell.

Dry earth —
Bare trees —
Frozen soil —
Cold air —
Cold water —
The beauty of winter.

Nature's call

The moon is full,
The night air so cool.
I hear wolves' howls,
The hooting of the owls,
The cold fresh breeze from the sea,
The whispering wind from a tree,
The pathless path under the forest,
The flowing babbling brook never at rest,
The blurring lonely hills,
The dim lake sitting still,
The melancholy sound of a waterfall,
Is it Nature's call to me?

S. Siangshai

Take me to a small Isle

Take me to a small isle
Where my weary soul can rest awhile.
Alone in silence and tranquility,
Away from society.

Where only Peace will be my medicine,
To repent for all my sins.
Where by day, I'll sit by the shore,
Composing poetry from my *deep heart's core.*
And by night, on the strand of that small land,
I'll lay my head on the soft sand;
With fire on the side,
I'll lend my ears to the tide,
And my eyes will gaze at the stars,
While sipping on some whiskey.

I am Black and White

I am Black and White,
I am a Dove if you show Love,
And a Devil if you show Evil,
I am Dr. Jekyll and Mr. Hyde.

I am sweet like a honey bee,
Salty like the sea,
And bitter like a neem tree.

I am both: the lightning and the thunder's
powerful blow,
And the fascinating colorful rainbow.
I am a master of Disaster.
I am a master of Wonder.

I am like the ocean's wave
Without patience, I'll come at full pace.
Don't push me.

I can be a candle's light in the dark,
And the Evil that comes at night when the dogs
bark.

I am the Earthquake
That can make you shake
Till you stumble and crumble.

S. Siangshai

Ode to Isolation

Why I feel so belong here, at Isolation?
That is filled with cold, smoke and damnation.
Where emotions take over
And the pen gain power.
Where I see only calamity
And yet, the sound of silence brings tranquility.
There is no home for me here
But there is comfort
And comfort is most found at home.
Even though it kills to be here
Don't think I feel fear
This place treats me like a Dear.

My only friends in this place are Black Pen and
Blank Paper,
They persuade me to be a better writer.
And so my *Black* side embraces this place
As this place provides space,
For my taste in writing
And scribbling words from my thoughts.
But my other side wishes not to face this place.

Black and Blank asked: *Don't you feel free here?*
My other side replied: *Its Darkness.*
Art is born out of it but without happiness.
They said: *You might as well face it now*

Later, in your tomb, there is only doom.
Don't think it's the same as in the womb.

S. Siangshai

She Smiled

She stood on the sundeck
That views to the blue sea;
The hills and setting sun.
She lights a cigarette;
Puff, puff, puff and she paused.
Frozen in her deep thoughts
As tears filled up her eyes,
She bends her head downward;
Like a dying flower
Just waiting for the wind
To take her far away.

What thoughts circulate through her brain?
What thoughts does she hold that made her
froze?
Is it the death of her loved ones?
Or is it fear that has seized her?
What pain she bear? No one knows.

Between her shivering fingers;
The cigarette slowly linger
As the smoke dances with the wind.
Just below the sundeck
There is a fragile tree
Left with only one last young leave;
Holding on to its little branch.

She watches the last leave shivers;
Persisting not to fall
And get carried away
By the force of the wind.
Hours passed, the leave still on its branch,
Captivated by it, she smiled.

Jumping to the Unknown

Jumping to the unknown,
Journeying alone on my own,
Always urging to explore the unknown.

I've jumped to the darkest and deepest depth of
an ocean,
I've jumped to places with great depression and
obsession,
I've jumped to a place where Mephistopheles
resided when none could see,
I've jumped to places that pictured hell
Where only void and darkness dwell.

But now, it seems I have jumped into a trap,
Into a newly dug grave
That is not meant for me.
I was brave but now I crave to be saved.

The Devil in my mind

"Temptation is the Devil's greatest arsenal."

I spoke to the Devil —
Last night — in the dark;
It was past midnight.

He was a gentleman
But not a virtuous man.
He was pale and fair,
With bright flaming eyes,
And words full of lies.

He had no horns
But he was a Tempter,
Like Eden's snake.

He talked of murder,
Money and Power.
And gave his attention
To anyone alone,
With evil intentions.
He chooses no one,
But welcomes anyone
Who wishes for a throne.

He feeds his slaves with Greed,
And leaves them with a hole,
For he takes out their soul.

I asked: Who created you?
Speak only what is true.
Religion! The Bible -
Carved me to credible.

Somewhere in a Small Village

Somewhere in a small village,
In a quiet and pleasant cottage,
With sparrows chirping on the roof,
A small window that views a kloof,
Is where I long to be
While sipping fragrant tea.

In the pastoral place of my childhood days,
Where tomorrow is the same as today;
Where the sky is filled with birds catching their
prey;
Where fire in a small hearth never dies;
Where fair maidens rest under a shady tree
And flutter when young men pass by;
And life, like a turtle, just goes by.

S. Siangshai

She was a Shooting Star

She was a bright shooting star
Whom everybody missed while making a wish.
She was a small slippery fish
Who slides away from anybody's radar.

She was young, green and sprouting,
Like someone born out of spring.
Once, I saw her with a heart-broken look,
Her tears flowed like a babbling spring's brook.
It was the saddest admiration,
That then put my heart in ignition.

She was like the moon,
Who doesn't always stay full,
But with every shape she was beautiful —
And that kept her Romeos in a swoon.

She glittered like gold
When sunlight sat on her skin,
Her Romeos would urge to win her
Even if it meant to sin —
All — in pursuit to get hold of her.

She was a shooting star
Who liked to disappear into an unimaginable
place,
Or maybe into another space —
Leaving her admirers with a scar.

S. Siangshai

While the World turns into Chaos

A cigarette burning slowly —
Amidst the sparkling starry night —
With a woeful melodic tune from a bird —
Who wants to be heard —
The warm gentle touch of the passing breeze —
And the gentle whispering trees —
Compose for thy unstable mind to be at peace.
While the world turns into chaos —
Alone, I'll watch thee without pathos!

A peek into the life of a Shepherd

Often times a wish to know
Come forth and go
In thy empty thirsty mind
Of what thoughts entangles behind
A Shepherd's mind.

In thy wakeful sleep
Million miles of imagination I'd keep
On a Shepherd's life
Who never did strive
For an ambitious life.

One divine sunny day
I saw him sat with grace
On a fine suitable rock
While his obedient flock
At their routine state – graze
And I from a distant – just gaze

He took out his instrument
Played to his inanimate greeny audience
From deep his heart with confidence
Which left them all in merriment.
They all bend towards this majestic play
Just when the surprising wind invited them to
dance;

An inevitably undeniable chance.
They moved rhythmically in gay
As if showing their gratitude for the skilled artist
Who seemed to have set his spirit at bliss.

When the music is no more loud
And the grass, no more than a silent crowd
He was solitarily without a friend
And I sadly wonder at that moment
If he ever has a friend?

O Soft wind

O soft wind, come not harshly,
Nor with sad and tragic news,
But soothingly and steadily,
For this day is too lively to add bruise.
This day, this place,
Calm as the sea at night,
Filled with earth's greenery sights,
And the bright, balmy celestial sky
That keeps the spirits high —
Is a cup of fortune for thy endless misfortune.

So come now and gently sweep us off this
sorrow;
A sorrow that we'll not carry to tomorrow.

S. Siangshai

Are we who we really are?

Are we who we really are?
When truly we are influenced
To become who we are now,
Based on the characters we admire
And who truly inspire us.
We dedicate to imitate —
Our-Self as other characters —
Fictional or non-fictional.
And so there lays within us —
Mixed, multiple characters
That play our regular role,
Which drives us towards our goal
And yet leaves us in contradiction
Of our true Self. Because now —
We are an influenced perception
Of our admired characters.

Some turn monster —
Some murderer —
Some powerful —
Some ordinary.

In truth, we are just like flowers
Fragile and weak, we are born
When wither, we disperse and gone
Some leave seeds, some don't.

And each holds our own kind of beauty
That blooms somewhere amidst our frailty.

S. Siangshai

An incurable Sadness

As darkness lurks in
And your heart I can never win
In this pitiful slow passing night
I'm left and turn to a terrible sight.

An incurable sadness grips me,
I sit pondering upon the moon
Fantasizing about you and me—
I almost fall into a swoon.

In this foolish pursuit of love
Is there a remedy to move on?
To make this incurable sadness gone.
Is there no remedy for this disease?

In this dreary hour of sadness
I've found fantasy to be the *Ecstasy* to euphoria.

Poem of the Dead

I know it is not okay
To leave you all this way.
I did not bid you all goodbye
Partly because I did not want to die.
But I heard my absurd Calling,
From God or Mister Death, I do not know
I only knew it was time to go.

When I look back to see where I have reached,
I am sadly happy as I write this at the beach.
I watch the sunset, reminiscing upon it;
The memories behind have all been sweet.
So, weep not nor let your heart ache,
Live on to the fullest for my sake.
Let not my death be a burden
For I am now at peace in the Silent Garden,
Among our kin and ancestors —
Eternally alive in death,
With frozen breath.
Remember me and I'll always be in your heart,
Even though we are now forever apart.

S. Siangshai

Glimme and the Sparrows

Glimme had two Sparrows
Locked inside a small thin cage
That stood beside an undying rose;
She named them June and Moon;
For June, she sings only in June,
And Moon only when there's a full moon.

Glimme is like *the Frog who's stuck in a well,*
And likes to think all is well.
She is a wounded soul with little hope,
Hanging at the end of the rope.
Her life is a cycle of day and night
Like a clock – same pattern and rhythm, rotating
in plight.

With the Sparrows, she finds herself at ease
And her uneasy mind at peace,
Although the birds weren't much active
But were lovely and all but attractive.

One autumn, she finally set the Sparrows free
Without hesitation, they went on to flee.
And though the clock goes round and round,
Change has just begun to sow its seed in the
ground —
For Glimme.
With time, she became a little more cheerful

When she saw the Sparrows free and joyful.
It was then she knew – tomorrow
Will no more bring her sorrow.

Illusion

In the end,
Only my imaginary friend
Who can soothe the perplexity of thy heart and
mind,
Leaving all of reality behind.

She's my lulling lullaby;
Who never bids me goodbye.

They say that Life goes on

They say that life goes on
But here in our small town,
I fear it seems to have stopped.
Ev'ry week, there's a body
To bury in the ground.
And the people that still live —
Are living an absurd life.

The children, the young and the old
Are all lost in bewilderment.
The children have stopped being bold
And have lost touch with merriment.
The young ones roam about the street —
With deceiving smiles on their faces,
Unemployed and barely living;
They have forgotten their passion.
The old sit at home and worry —
About their blurry memory,
And complain about making a change,
Yet do nothing to bring a change.

Just the other day, I saw —
A half-witted drunken man
Walk 'round a dry field aimlessly
Till he collapsed under a tree.

His wife had died nine years ago;
Since then, he has been a shipwreck.

They say that life goes on
But here in our small town,
Everybody's in a breakdown.

Growing up

In my olden days
Or should I say, my golden days,
I knew no stress – only happiness.
As a free little child,
I ran 'round the streets free and wild.
There was none to stop me,
Except for my two allied enemies:
Which were Age and Time,
Who didn't severely pose a threat at the time.

Soon, as I grow up,
My freedom with it drops.
I used to drink from a running stream,
Now it's only in my daydream.
I used to fly kites,
But now I'm the government's kite.
Exposed to the system,
I am chained to it.

S. Siangshai

The Village Kids

Every spring, our village kids
They will go on chasing rabbits
Without slippers on their feet.
Like an active newborn deer;
They run and play wild without fear.
Every day was a bright beautiful day
Their only wish was for it to stay that way.

Every summer, they go for a swim;
Catch fishes by a small stream—
Lie on sands and daydream.
And like a pack of wolves
They will hunt deep in the woods,
Climb trees like monkeys,
And feed their belly with berries
Until it filled their empty bellies.

Every autumn, they would have that mischievous
smiled
As they became a little wild.
Their heart was never at calm,
Like squirrels they like to steal from farmer's
farm
And rode on a mine's tram;
In a euphoric mood—
Down the hills to a small dam;

Where they would intentionally ram.
Not a single autumn's day goes without their
enjoy,
As the season filled their lives with overjoy.

Every winter, they would roam
And wants to never return home.
Dressed in rags—
Hands and feet covered in black—
Dusty hair—
From dusty air—
With blazing eyes—
They would follow a lone herdsman;
To hear his fascinating folktales.
And they would tease young women—
Carrying water from the dales.
They would gamble with marbles—
Play hide and seek,
Once or twice a week—
Compete in flying kites—
Cursed the winner with foolish spells.
And when the day has gone,
They trail back home singing a song.

O, Sweet Summer Days

O, lonely water, where do you flow hereafter?
O, heart soothing breeze, where do you wander?
O, endless happiness, do you even exist?
Because if you do, my heart wants you seized.

O, sweet summer days,
Won't you pass by at a snailing pace?
I want this feeling to last awhile,
So, I can hold on a little longer to this smile.

On Sadness

*"O Sadness, won't you offer me a crumb of
Happiness?"*

Sadness, you and me are meant to be,
I am chained to you and you to me,
You always find your way back to me
And I to you —
You're like an embraceable flu,
It's hard to escape you.

You've consumed my all,
Now I'm on the Fall
And Death is the only Call —
Yet I will stand tall —
Death is no escape but more bitter sorrow,
YOU of all should know.

S. Siangshai

Sadness, *dear*

What is happy without knowing Sadness?
What is Sad without knowing Happiness?

Today, was an ecstatic day
Now, I lay ruminating upon it.
My cup cannot hold such happiness no more
So, Sadness dear or should I call you lurker,
Come now, and give me the heartsore.

Happiness has only given me temporary joy
But you, you taught me to cherish rain
Even when I'm holding so much pain
And taught me to appreciate solitude
Even when in the saddest mood.

Before I lay me to Eternal Sleep

Before I lay me to eternal sleep
Bless my loved ones never weep
And memories of me they'll always keep.

Before my time runs out
Pray I've made few proud
And that my name will go clear and loud.

Before Death walk down the aisle
Pray I look at her with a smile
Knowing I've lived and the next journey will be
worthwhile.

Before I rest my soul
Pray I've staged well my role
And as a living being, I've reached my goal.

S. Siangshai

My Love

My love,
All you hold is cigarettes and regrets
My love,
Our spark had died
When you first lied
My love,
You shouldn't have kept all those dark secrets

Roses and cakes
Patch up and breaks
Look at us now, shattered—
Our hearts covered in snowflakes

My love,
You broke your promise
Surely, you will be missed
My love,
A Muse – you used to be
Now you're just another memory

So much for a happy plan
Only to land on a tragic end.

The echo of Duitara

Where are the songs of Duitara?
Aye, where are they brother-sister?
The song our forefathers loved —
The song that speaks for us —
The song from a Duitara's heart.

Are we so lost and manipulated by the Westerns
That we have forgotten where we come from?
When did we get this far?
In the midst of gaining our freedom,
We have kept aside our wisdom
That was instilled in us by our forefathers.
Looking at us now from their grave,
At how we have become enslaved,
They will probably sigh thinking —
Where will we go from here?

The Outsiders may have taken everything
But not our identity.
Our forefathers had not fought and bled
Only for us to forget.
They fought – so we could keep our Identity.
We have come a long way,
So, don't you dare throw all that away.

Be ashamed not of who we were,

But of our children when they stop to care.
So, I call upon you, brother-sister,
To play on the songs of Duitara —
The songs that tell our stories,
The songs that emotionally bind our hearts.

Duitara: A Khasi traditional instrument.

Drooping Dying Grass

Drooping dying grass,
Sigh not, this is not your last.
You've weathered every storm
And have displayed your class and form.

A short silent evil wintry attack, now —
Shall not let your spirit lack.
You've planted your roots strong,
And that is enough for you to survive long.

You may wither and fall
But you shall not die at all
For spring will soon be here
So have no more fear.

And when spring arrives
From the ground, your new leaves shall strive —
Green and elegant, wearing diamond-like dews
With such a fine state for one to muse.

You are an unnoticed piece of beauty.

O beauty, shimmering flower,
Will you not stay the same forever?
O sweet soft melodic whispering wind,
Keep pace and let her dance to your melody.

The End!